BETH SCOTT

Postcards from Hell: Vol 1

A Horror Anthology

Copyright © 2022 by Beth Scott

All rights reserved. No part of this publication may be reproduced, stored or transmitted in any form or by any means, electronic, mechanical, photocopying, recording, scanning, or otherwise without written permission from the publisher. It is illegal to copy this book, post it to a website, or distribute it by any other means without permission.

This novel is entirely a work of fiction. The names, characters and incidents portrayed in it are the work of the author's imagination. Any resemblance to actual persons, living or dead, events or localities is entirely coincidental.

Beth Scott asserts the moral right to be identified as the author of this work.

First edition

This book was professionally typeset on Reedsy.
Find out more at reedsy.com

Contents

Billy's Golden Light	1
The Babysitter	4
A Bad Night for It	7
Skin Deep	13
No Good, No Good	22
The A4	27
New Patio	30
The River Killer	33
Undone	37
In the Streetlight	40
Corpse #2	42
The Red Man	47
The Flogsta Scream	51
About the Author	53

Billy's Golden Light

Billy was big, slow, and gentle. Everybody at school liked him… except a couple of kids, but his mum said that was normal.

He was polite to girls, and helped people when they fell over. And when Kacie Gutteridge found a dead pigeon by the oak tree at the edge of the sports field, Billy heard her crying and squeezed his fists and shut his eyes and thought very hard of a golden light. The pigeon flopped onto its pink legs, ruffled its feathers and scrambled into the air, making Kacie shriek with fright and relieved laughter and happiness.

Kacie liked Billy a lot after that. Not *like*-liked. Billy cared more about being *liked*. About people seeing that soft, golden light in him. So when Kacie whispered to Marcia, and they went out and found a squirrel in the road, but its head was squashed, and they snuck it into school in a shoebox, Billy said no. Marcia said he was lying. But she was even more sad when her cat died a week later, so he did something nice for her. All was forgiven.

That was why Craig pushed him over. It really hurt.

'You're a witch,' Craig said. 'You need to die. Stop being creepy, the girls don't like it.'

Billy hoped this was a lie. He was always careful to help people because that stopped him being scared of himself.

'Craig's just acting out,' Billy's mum told him that evening. 'What he did was wrong, but you need to be nice, sweetheart. Remember, Craig doesn't have a mum.'

Yes he does, thought Billy. *Liar.* And that poisonous blob in Billy's mind grew and grew, all the way 'til eleven o' clock, until he threw back his sheets and told the poison, 'Time to go.'

Billy was good at silently opening the front door, because he did it once a week. And Billy's parents never suspected it because they liked him. He was careful to keep them liking him.

The cold air felt like an exciting secret, and Billy walked as quick as a lick. He found the grey stone wall and wiggled through the gate.

It took a lot of finding. He couldn't remember Craig's last name. But he found the new part of the graveyard, and among the gnomes and pinwheels and shining black headstones he saw Craig's handwriting on a slumped-over, soggy card and lilies that spelled out M-U-M.

Billy clenched his fists, and summoned the golden light. After a while, he felt the weight lift and stopped holding his breath. Nothing but silence.

Then, a scratch.

A low murmur, which grew to a muffled shriek, and scratching like a dog wanting to be let in.

It was loud, so Billy watched for lights in the houses over the wall. A big thump in the ground made a blue pinwheel fall over. He backed off—could she get out? He wondered if she had fake fingernails on, and if they broke off. He wondered if it hurt. The scratching got less. He didn't hear the voice any more.

Billy held his breath, watching, for ten minutes. Nothing happened, so he decided to go home.

In the morning, his first smell was eggs.

'Hi! Sleep well?' His mum had a big smile.

Billy nodded happily, feeling peaceful as his mum gave him a plate of scrambled eggs, a one-armed squeeze and a kiss on the head.

'I love you, honey.'

Billy liked to be loved. And going to the graveyard some once a week helped him like others a little more.

The Babysitter

It was a sharp, bright night in October, and Amy hugged her cardigan tight around her as the Kendricks recited their instructions on the front step.

'There's half a tub of raspberry ripple in the freezer,' Mrs Kendrick said. 'He won't make a peep—but just in case, the number's on the fridge.'

'We'll be fine.' Amy smiled.

Mr Kendrick took his wife's arm. 'We'll be back around midnight. And don't open the door, I mean it. There's some real weirdos around here.'

'Oh, I won't.' Amy promised. 'Have a ton of fun!' And she meant it, waiting until Mrs Kendrick got in the car before closing the front door softly.

The house—with its vanilla-wax-melt, clean-laundry, new-carpet scent—was hers.

It filled her lungs for a second, and she exhaled with decadent satisfaction. School was in a downward spiral and her parents were fighting worse than ever. She needed tonight: and she had been *soooo* looking forward to indulging herself.

On the way to the kitchen, the cream, plush carpet sinking deliciously under the feet of her school tights, Amy hummed a tune and opened the cupboards one by one, just to look.

At the back door, a black figure ducked under the window.

Pulling open a drawer, Amy froze. Did she hear something? After a couple seconds, she thought better of it. She bumped her hip on the drawer and closed it over the gleaming knives within, and grabbed some crackers instead.

Turning, she saw a man wearing a black balaclava standing in the living room.

It happened in seconds. Amy yanked the drawer back open and grabbed the butcher knife as the man lunged to grab her, crackers smashing into the carpet as she scrambled past him.

I've got to get upstairs... the baby!

Swinging at him, finally getting free, Amy fell onto the staircase. 'Get away from me!'

Cold air brushed her neck from the open front door as her slippery feet propelled her up the stairs. The man grabbed at her, his fist empty—she reached the landing at last, his footsteps thundering behind her, and turned to see three other black-garbed men crowding the hallway.

Amy threw herself at the doors—there were five, she couldn't remember which was the nursery—and as the men got closer, she madly slashed, keeping them at bay. Finally, she heard the baby, woken up from the noise.

I've got to get him!

She threw herself into the room and tripped, falling on her front with her arm outstretched towards the baby wailing in his crib, as the intruders crowded the landing.

'Police! Drop your weapon!'

Amy craned her neck over her shoulder to see the men in black frozen in the doorway, staring at her.

'Fuck you,' she growled, groping for her weapon. With a feral yell, Amy scrambled off the floor and brought the knife down over the crib—a gunshot exploded her chest, scarlet blooming over the nursery's cream carpet, echoing into the street.

The Kendricks were already outside, intermittently lit by blue and red lights, and let out a howl when they heard the noise. But when they heard their baby's cry a moment later, horror gave way to relief.

'She looked so nice,' Mr Kendrick muttered into his wife's hair, over and over. 'She looked so... *normal.*'

A Bad Night for It

The White Hart Inn had a warm glow in its black-wood belly, thick and soft against the chill, moonlit night outside.

Twisting a rag in a glass, I glanced at the clock above the slumped shoulder of our last regular. Five past eleven.

'Lock in tonight, Ted?'

The regular's baleful eyes met mine, and he gripped his pint. Nodding slowly, he seemed to shrink in deference. *If you would, Leah,* his wet paper bag stance said. He dug his fingers into the wet corners of his eyes. *Please.*

'Wonderful idea.' Jerry, the landlord, came out of the back room with a fresh box of crisps and started stuffing handfuls into the basket on show. 'Not a good night to be out.'

I tiptoed for the keys on their brass hook, and glanced at Ted. A damp sniff escaped from the gaps in his fingers. His hand was over his face. Remembering his wife.

The door burst open. 'Help! Come quickly—please!' There stood a young guy around my age, and I wouldn't have said no. His shirt had been ironed that night, now heavily creased. The cold air snuck its fingers in around him, teasing hints of expensive cologne.

I froze. Ted didn't turn round, but Jerry squared his fists and asked what happened.

The new guy's eyes shot around the empty bar. 'It's... God, it's so bad, please... there was an accident and my girlfriend got hurt...'

I glanced at Jerry. His face was grey and blank as a new gravestone.

'Please!' The new guy's voice pitched. 'You've got to know first aid, I've got no signal out here, it's only up the road!'

'Where?' I said.

'I don't know, about half a mile maybe? Up the lane. We were heading this way.'

Jerry grabbed the landline. 'I'll call 999.'

The young guy went white. 'N-no... she needs help, now! An ambulance won't get here in time—'

Jerry shook his head. 'We don't go out,' he told him. 'Not on nights like this.'

Fear, revulsion and anger passed over the other guy's face in waves. 'What do you mean?' he cried. 'She's dying!'

'Close the door, please.'

'Just help me!'

'Close that door right now,' Jerry bellowed, 'or that thing which jumped in front of your goddamn car is going to get in here!'

There was silence. It was like the safe warmth in the White Hart took a breath and bulged outward, keeping the blue cold outside the open door at bay.

'How did you...?'

'Was it a child?' I asked him, morbidly curious. 'A big deer, or your mother?'

The stranger looked at me, his lovely green eyes scarred with fright. 'I thought... looked like a deer, at first.'

Ted snorted, downing the last of his pint.

I regarded my employer. 'We can't just leave her out there, Jer.'

Flexing the tendons in his jaw, the big man gave me a look that said, *What if there isn't any of her left?*

'Go for it,' slurred Ted, to the foam in his empty glass. 'I didn't, but you folks might get lucky. I'll keep a watch here.'

There was a shotgun mounted above the bar, amongst a constellation of horse brass and replica flagons. It was not for show.

* * *

Jerry placed the shotgun and a cardboard box of ammo in the bed of his truck, and the young man and I squeezed in the front. Up close, his cologne was sweet, daubed on a patch of rough shaven neck. He frantically told Jerry where to head.

'It was already a bad night,' the stranger went on, landing his forehead on the cold window. 'She wasn't interested. I was acting an idiot, showing off. And that... that thing might have killed her.'

'You're not the first,' I said, wanting to fill the silence, make him feel better. 'Started a couple years ago. It was in the papers. A guy beat his wife into a coma, left her tied her up in the lane. Hardly anyone uses it—maybe twice a day each way? It was a tractor, didn't see her. That's when it started.' I thought about Ted, alone in the pub. 'It—she, the curse, her revenge, whatever—it makes itself look like what you want most. Not enough to arouse suspicion, of course. It's never appeared as a celebrity, or a pile of money or anything. Just something you want. It usually looks like dead people. Just enough to make you get out of the car and look around on that road.'

Condensation from the stranger's—I never asked his name—clammy forehead ran down the window as he looked at me.

'Oh, yeah? What did you see?'

No good conversation followed, so we fell into silence. The single-lane road had hedges on either side, and our view was limited to three feet at 25 mph for several minutes until the stranger sat up, excited. 'The postbox,' he said. 'Here—it's up here, on the left.'

A lump of nausea sat high in my stomach as we drew closer to the vehicle, half-swallowed by hedgerow and pitched into the verge. The passenger door was open.

'You stay here,' Jerry growled, flicking on the hazard lights as he and the stranger got out.

I shifted to the middle of the seat. With a clatter from the truck bed, Jerry got the shotgun. The stranger ran towards the car, shouting what I guess was his girlfriend's name.

Watching the headlights was like a stage play: the strange man looked in the car, then walked round it, shouted, and put his hands on his head. 'Where is she?' Our hero Jerry enters from stage right, shotgun pointed into the gloom. 'Oh, Jesus...'

I saw a shining slick of blood under his shoes as the stranger danced to and fro. It led from the passenger door of his wrecked car across the road to a break in the other hedge. I hammered my fist on the windscreen and pointed at it.

Jerry saw. 'Get inside, now!'

But the strange man whirled around, as if he'd heard something. He screamed his date's name and ran down the road, out of the headlights.

'Damn it!'

On instinct, I grabbed a tyre iron Jerry keeps in his driver's side door and tumbled out. 'Shoot it!'

Jerry hesitated. I could see it. I reached him as he called out into the darkness, a name I didn't recognise.

'The hell?' I hissed. 'Get back in the truck, it's out there!'

A moony, far-off look was in Jerry's eyes. 'I'll shoot it, I promise,' he muttered. 'I just want to see her.'

As he took a few steps towards the edge of the headlights, I lurched to him. 'Give me your keys—your goddamn keys, Jerry!' Wrestling them from the ring on his belt buckle, he flinched away with disgust, like I was insignificant. I didn't care. I scrunched the cold keys safe in my fist. That's when it ran out of the shadows and sank its teeth into Jerry's shoulder.

The air exploded in a bright flash as the shotgun fell to the road and blasted a hole in the wrecked car. I threw myself at the truck. Groping for the door handle, my vision was a too-bright mess of stars and headache. Jerry groaned loudly, over the soggy noise of his innards being dragged over the tarmac.

I climbed into the driver's seat, the keys in my lap, frantically sorting them with my eyes squeezed mostly shut.

Her. He just wanted to see her?

Jerry's sister was a hundred miles away, dying in hospital. *Jerry, you idiot.*

I found it. Wrenching the key in the ignition, the engine rumbled into life—and then it was at my window, the glass reverberating with force.

'Help... it's out here!' It was the young man with the green eyes, pounding on the glass. My fingers went to the door handle, but I stared. Blood was soaking into his nice shirt...

...All the way up to his mouth.

Yeah. Only then it hit me.

In a moment that seemed like forever, last week's supermarket routine played in my mind. He'd been in the tea and coffee aisle, with a basket of single man's food. Had that nice shirt on, contemplating dark roast with those green eyes. I lingered, watching. Imagined taking home and kissing the bloodied mouth that now grinned at me through the window. Laughing with him, and sharing the day's events.

How lonely was I? It chose *him*.

'Fuck you,' I screamed, threw the truck into reverse, and backed away so hard that creature wearing the skin of my supermarket crush stumbled. My golden headlights lit him up, from the scarlet gore down his front to his etched-relief stubble and the green of his furious eyes that filled up with the front of the truck as I slammed down my foot.

The bonnet crumpled like foil under his outstretched hands and, like a rag doll, he went under. I landed back in my seat, glancing in the rear view mirror. Something large, broken and black dragged its scaly leg back into the rushing shadows.

I didn't want to open the windows. The cool night air smelled dangerous and alarming to me… and the seat upholstery still held traces of his cologne.

Skin Deep

On my foot? God's sake, not my foot. Not tonight. I need to sleep, I thought, flinging my sweat-soaked sheets against the wall and limping across the hallway. I switched on the bathroom light, squeezing my eyes shut against the fluorescent onslaught. Pulsing my weight from one tender foot to the other, I splashed cold water on my face to slough off the fatigue.

Oh, are you gonna look down? Expect to see something so soon?

I rubbed the towel over my eyes, peeking over the fuzzy edge at my two same old feet.

Nothing.

I staggered back to bed, switching the light off and leaning against the wall for a second. I grabbed the towel from the hook, wrapping it around myself as I fell onto my mattress, trying to ignore the painful sensation. As if my right foot had pins and needles, only ten times worse. White noise under my skin.

A few hours later, I dragged myself into work.

'She... was... so... funny and... kind,' a woman was sobbing, cradled by her husband. I was holding a styrofoam cup of black coffee under my nose, praying the invigorating aroma would wake me up more.

'I'm sorry for your loss,' I repeated. 'This is just a formality.

As soon as we get the signature we can get everything moving forwards. Now, you've already mentioned your daughter's septum piercing and a scar behind her right ear, which will be enough for a positive identification. What about the tattoo?'

'Tattoo?' the husband said, in a small voice. I winced, knowing I'd divulged the poor girl's secret. It hadn't been done by a steady hand, and she was only 16. A friend probably did it.

'I'll show you now,' I said gently. 'Everything's ready.'

You get used to the wailing. I'd heard it only once before I started work at the morgue, as a young paramedic attending a road crash. The mother of the victim turned up and saw his mangled face smeared across the front of the car where he'd went over. Earring got caught on the wiper. A loved one's howl echoes, freezing everyone at the scene. My colleague mentioned matter-of-factly that you never get used to it.

Thing is, you do at the morgue. It's often the first time loved ones see the deceased, when it really sinks in. The horror, the urgency, for them is just the same as by the roadside—especially if it's messy. Maybe it's because I've heard so many now. Maybe it's because I feel safe in the lab: I'm not in the middle of the road, in among mangled metal in the snow shining with red and blue lights.

I strategically folded back the sheet to show them the septum piercing, and then the scar. They stated that yes, that was their daughter, no question. I then proceeded to fold back the sheet over the foot of the corpse, and show them the blurry blue outline of—a cat? A heart? The mother said nothing. The father chuckled, sadly.

'She never listened.'

I was washing up for lunch when Michelle poked her head around the door. 'We've just had one come in,' she said, and paused. 'There's a powder for that, you know.'

I'd been stamping, scraping the top of my foot with the heel of my shoe. 'Sock fell down,' I said. I plunged my hands back into the sink, out of view. 'Need me now?'

'No. It'll do after you eat. And pull up your sock.'

'What's the COD?'

'Motorcycle accident,' she said, turning to leave. 'He was in one of those gangs.'

My heart sank a mile.

I slammed the door to the bathroom stall behind me, rifling in my bag as I sat heavily on the toilet. Pulling out my sandwich and my notebook, I found the tube of cream I keep hidden in the bottom pocket, wrapped in a scarf. I kicked off my shoe—it smacked into the door—and ripped off my sock.

The top of my foot was an angry scarlet, flaking skin peeling off to reveal a hazy, sapphire outline. Brighter than hers—after all, mine was new.

I swore under my breath. I'd heard of teenagers doing this with sewing needles and ballpoint ink. If I got an infection, I'd really be pissed, and I couldn't even sue. No one would believe me. I squeezed the cream straight on, lathering the soothing cool solution onto my raw skin, massaging out the soreness. *Huh, it was a heart.* It was still visible under the oily white slick, like a drowning victim.

After washing my hands and eating my sandwich, I felt slightly more human. Just enough to get on with the job, until was reminded with a peal of dread of who was for the next post-mortem.

'That is some art project.' Michelle clicked her tongue, impressed, as we peeled back the sheet. The guy was in his mid-forties, covered head to toe in misty primary colours and symbols.

'Are you fucking kidding me,' I muttered. My skin was already beginning to crawl in anticipation of another sleepless night.

'Judgmental, much?' Michelle raised an eyebrow. 'I think they're expressive.'

'No, it's just,' I swallowed. 'What a waste. You know?'

She hmm'd in agreement, and thankfully didn't push the subject. 'Looks like a pretty clean hit. Hey look, knuckle dusters, like yours.' She held up his right fist, emblazoned with script letters. 'What does yours say?'

I clenched my own fist under the table. Usually I wore two pairs of gloves, but we'd run out. She would have spotted the outlines under the latex. 'Love and hate,' I muttered.

'Wow. So original.' She rolled her eyes. 'Come on, we need to get this guy processed. His friends are coming to ID him in an hour.'

Michelle went to have her own lunch when we were done, leaving me to finish up and await the loved ones. I didn't mind. With Michelle it was always tears and hugs, but I'd developed a penchant for deadpan delivery and zero emotion not long after I started having sleepless nights.

I heard the doors open, and went into the hallway to be greeted by the sight of half a dozen biker ogres in black jackets covered in patches. I was strangely touched. Most of them looked spooked as hell.

'Afternoon gentlemen,' I said.

The leader greeted me with an upward nod. 'We're here for Bill.'

'It's pretty open and shut,' I explained. 'I'm sorry for the a formality. Thank you for coming.'

The leader sniffed his nose. 'I'm Ed, that's Roger, Paul, Mike,

Tobs and Dave. What happens now?'

'I'll take you in to view the body,' I said, 'and then we'll need a few signatures. Then we can release him probably before midday tomorrow morning. Did Bill have a partner, or family?'

'Just us,' said Ed, in a tone of voice that sounded like a brick wall. My respect for him increased.

'Then let's go,' I said, and led them into the room.

The bikers, pale and shaken, arranged themselves around the gurney. Once they were ready, I slowly rolled back the body's sheet to the waist. These guys weren't howlers. Just a sharp intake of breath, and a few wet swallows. I could see Ed steel himself, a tendon in his jaw flexing hard.

'That's Bill,' he said, nodding quickly. 'His favourite rugby club. And his mother's name—she's dead. And he liked Bruce Lee movies, so he got a tiger.' He pointed at the corresponding tattoos on the corpse's chest.

'We were admiring the work,' I said. 'It's fantastic. Really.' I scratched the top of my foot with my other heel. I'd need to put more cream on soon.

One of the others—Paul, I think—nudged their leader. 'Bill had a special tattoo, one that meant a lot to us, on his right hand. Can you show us that one?'

I jerked out of my daydream, wondering which of Bill's lovely works of art were going to manifest on my swollen, sweaty knuckles somewhere around midnight, and told him yes, absolutely. I'd picked up Bill's limp hand when meaty fingers clamped around my own wrist.

'Take your glove off,' snapped the skinny one, Tobs.

'No,' I exclaimed, too astounded to wriggle out of his grip.

'Ed,' Tobs said urgently, not letting go. Ed frowned at me, then looked down at my hand holding the dead man's.

'Take it off,' said Ed, in a low voice.

'I'm afraid I can't,' I said, 'health and safety prohibits—'

'Now.'

'Fine,' I said, then I turned to glare at Tobs. 'Fine!' He let go, I gently placed the dead Bill's hand back down on the gurney. I peeled off my latex rubber glove, flexing my fingers and revealing fuzzy black outlines across my knuckles that had only appeared in the last half hour.

Ed stretched out an open hand over the corpse of their fallen comrade. I placed my hand in his, slowly.

'I know what it looks like,' I murmured. 'But I assure you, I have absolutely no idea—'

'You think you're hard or something?' Roger burst out.

'No, I—'

'Bloody joker...!'

'Shut up,' Ed snapped, and they fell silent.

It was the same. Exactly the bloody same. I recognised it the minute I saw the dead biker's hand: the exact same tattoo, on my own knuckles. I couldn't read it. It had come in too old. Of course, I'd been dreading this—the day I was etched with a bloody gang sign.

Ed looked at me. 'Where'd you get it?'

I hesitated. 'I didn't.' I figured the truth was better than a lie. 'It just appeared on me.'

To my shock, this wasn't questioned. 'When?'

'About six years ago.'

Ed's eyes—blue, misted by alcohol—locked onto mine for what felt like minutes. 'Do you recognise me?' he said, quietly.

'No, sir,' I said. 'I'm sorry.'

'Oh, I recognise you.' Ed let go of my hand and I drew it back in. 'See, you were there for our mate, Lester. At the end.'

Lester. The one whose earring got caught on the windshield wiper. He went over, smearing his face all over the gleaming blue hood of that car, a few awful seconds before rolling onto the road. I reached him first, just a young paramedic, and once my colleagues had detected a faint heartbeat I'd turned him over . He had no face, just a scarlet mush of gore and bone shards. I held his hand as they pushed tubes into his mouth. His eyes—shocked and wide—swivelled on me, one half-hidden under the scrap of a broken eyelid, and he squeezed my hand. Squeezed it hard. The tattooed letters had almost been scraped off his knuckles, but they were there. I couldn't sleep that night, after he died holding onto me. My hand was on fire. When I woke up, the letters were on me.

The others looked at their leader, incredulous. 'This is him?' Mike said.

'I don't understand,' I whispered.

'Letters are for leaders.' Ed clamped a massive hand on my shoulder. He held up his other fist, which was emblazoned with the same letters. Fresher on him, I could tell they spelled the gang's name. 'Lester was our leader. It wasn't no accident, he got run down by some bastards out for revenge. A centuries old revenge. See, these tattoos ain't... your usual kind.'

'Lester's mother did 'em,' said Paul.

'Lester and his mother were...' Ed paused for effect. 'Not your average people. See our tattoos, mine and Bill's, these are normal, like. Got 'em done in a shop. But they can't be passed on.'

'Passed on?' I repeated.

'You know what I mean.' Ed said. 'If you hadn't stepped in, if Lester had never given the tattoo to you, it would have passed to one of us. And we'd be next.'

'They can tell what's real,' Mike breathed.

'All of us would have died that night. One by one. If Lester hadn't stopped the tattoo from passing on. Kept it safe... on you.'

'So what's that?' I cried, pointing at his hand.

'It's a fake,' said Ed. 'See, we've got to keep up appearances. Got others that count on our rep. Bars, guys we protect. They'd notice, ask questions. But the man who ran down Lester? Those guys can tell it's not real. They see nothing more than ink. To them, we've not had a leader for years, and they all think we'll just die out. But now... right lads, is it time to finish it?'

The others nodded, sombre. 'Time to end 'em. For Lester. For Bill.'

Ed once again extended a hand to me, elbow down and palm open, like he wanted to arm wrestle. 'Time to give it back, mate,' he said. 'Don't be scared.'

I hesitated, trying to piece together the insane story I'd just heard. 'Will you be okay?'

Tobs nodded. 'We're ready.'

'It's been six years,' said Mike. 'Trust me. We've been waiting. Time to take these guys down for good.'

I flexed the fingers of my tattooed hand, and placed my palm in Ed's over the unmoving chest of the corpse on the gurney. 'Here goes nothing.'

Ed squeezed. Ed squeezed hard. And it shot a memory up my arm and into my cortex, of being on that cold road in the red and blue lights, staring into a mangled face and unquestioningly accepting a favour I was never aware of. I heard Lester's mother's howl, far off, through time and across miles, and my hand began to prickle with white noise.

A couple of moments later, it was over. Ed withdrew his hand,

and I looked at mine. The tattoo was gone. My knuckles were clean.

Grinning, the others gathered around Ed to look. The familiar letters on his own knuckles were crisp, fresh. Almost glowing.

'Thank you,' he nodded at me. 'You need anything from us—'

'Beer, protection...' said Tobs. 'Girls...'

I held up my new hands in protest. 'I'm fine,' I said. 'Honestly. All good.'

'I wasn't offering,' said Ed. 'This is for life. We're looking out for you, mate.'

I swallowed, unsure how good it was having these guys on my side. 'Appreciate it,' I told them anyway. 'It's no problem.'

They left, and I was alone with Bill's corpse. I raised my eyebrows at him, and wiped the sweat off my forehead. Then, suddenly, I remembered the rest of me. Yanking off my white coat, I hurriedly undid the buttons of my shirt and stared down at my chest and stomach. Bare. Naked and pink as a mole rat. No longer covered, overlapped and scarred with the tattoos of the hundreds of dead people who had passed through the morgue in the past six years, etched by unseen hands onto my skin at night. They'd all been passed on.

When I went home from work, I slept like the dead.

No Good, No Good

Going out to the field was getting to be a hassle.

As Ed packed his lunch (ham and cheese sandwich, no butter, one apple and a Coke) in the cool house, his gnarled fingers slipped. Knife took the tip clean off his pinky. Two cars made it down the dirt road like shining beetles skirting the horizon, in the fifteen minutes it took him to find a plaster that hadn't dried out and gather the dexterity to tear it out of its packet and wind it round the cut. He stuck it in his mouth and looked at the red spray over his sandwich. He'd eat it anyway, staring down the empty road. No good it going to waste.

The cut was healing, slow but sure. He didn't feel it: all that occupied his head was how the midday sun glared down his leathery neck and his bones grated as he walked out into the field, swinging the tin lunchbox, the gun inside clanking against the Coke.

'Mornin', Jenny.'

There was no reply. Out in the middle of the field, you could hear nothing. No trees, no birds. There was only the sun. Once in a while a breeze would make it over the wheat stubble and sway the scarecrow, drunkenly hoisted and nodding at his greeting like a drag queen Christ. Ed grabbed at the rainbow deck chair that was propped up beneath its skirt, threw it open, and set it onto a stable patch. He settled himself down to eat.

Minutes passed. Ed positioned himself so that Jenny's skirt tickled him so often, but didn't get in his eyes. Narrow, unblinking, the unlikely pair stared out at the dirt road as Ed chewed his sandwich. These days, Ed farmed dirt and not much else.

'Quiet today.' He got as much pleasure from Jenny's silence as he did her company. Sometimes she spoke to him, but today she was in a mood. Ed moved his gun off the second half of his sandwich. The barrel left a dent in the bread, but it stopped the cheese slipping out on the walk over.

Jenny, fat with straw and scantily clad in sun-bleached pink floral cotton, said nothing. Her eyes were bullet casings thumbed into a dried pumpkin.

'Yeah, nothin' much.'

Another quarter of an hour drifted by, and the pair said nothing. Ed took a sip of Coke. A buzzard landed on the far-off fence, but it didn't fancy the prospect of looking for mice in a dry field and carried on.

Ed heard the tyres first.

They crunched on the turning from smooth asphalt onto his road. A blue hatchback trundled along the horizon, left to right.

Ed's heart skittered. He got up, steadying himself on Jenny, with his gun stuffed into his back pocket and one hand staying on it. With the other, he waved.

The blue hatchback pulled to a stop. Ed's fingers tightened around the gun.

The doors opened, and two young men got out. One had a large folded map, and the other was looking at his smartphone. Their heads swung left and right, even upwards. Cartoonishly lost.

'Hello!' One of them spotted Ed and called over.

'Go back!' Ed's hand flapped like he was landing a plane.

The man's jaw hung slack, confused. 'Sorry?'

Ed gritted his teeth, shuffling uncomfortably into full sun. 'Not here!' he yelled. 'Back to the road!'

The second one looked over, having found no signal. His friend held up the map. 'Newsham?' he shouted, pointing down the road to Ed's farm.

'No!' Ed waved at him. 'Go back!'

Ed lost a little more hope in humanity as the men looked at each other, conferring in length about what this could possibly mean. They finally got the message, but they looked worried.

'Thanks,' called the first one. 'But if you see a red van…'

Ed shooed them off, and turned back to fuss with the lunchbox and gun on his deck chair.

The man hesitated, but eventually shrugged and he and his companion got in, did a three-point turn, and headed off back towards the road.

'No good, no good,' Ed muttered, fumbling with his things as he eventually collapsed back in his chair. 'No good tourists and city folk comin' round here, eh Jenny?'

The scarecrow did not reply.

Lastly, Ed ate the apple to calm his nerves. It cleansed his palate, and took off the fuzz of the Coke. He was quite content and pitched the core ten yards towards the fence when he saw the red van.

It rumbled along the dirt road, unreadable, and then stopped, engine idling. Ed licked his dry lips, and stroked his gun with a thumb. He'd fire a warning shot.

The driver's door opened, and the first thing he saw was

brown hair. Too long for a man, even a young one. She wore wide shorts, and he could hear her muttering once the breeze turned to him. Ed's heart started to hammer.

The girl looked over. Couldn't miss him. The only thing in that two acres apart from the farmhouse was yellow stubble, bright pink Jenny and grey old Ed in his rainbow chair. She raised a hand—not a hello, just an acknowledgement, a pause. She bent to rummage inside her vehicle. Ed swallowed.

The door slammed again, and the woman turned back with a map. 'Can you help me?'

Ed cupped his hand to his ear, barely an exaggeration. Without any complaint she planted her hands on the top bar of the fence and vaulted. She was walking over.

Ed stuffed the gun into his waistband and pulled his shirt over it. He tried to meet her halfway but the girl's pace outstripped him and they met in less than twenty paces.

Her face was friendly, up close, but she didn't smile. 'I'm wondering if you could help,' she said. 'I'm meeting friends in Newsham. Is this the turn-off?'

'No miss.'

The girl's face fell. 'I knew it,' she said. 'Look, was I supposed to take the right before or after this one?'

Ed wiped his forehead with the back of his wrist. 'Depends where you want to go,' he began, swaying. 'For the station it's... it's...'

'Oh, I'm sorry. Here.' The girl frowned. 'Let's get in the shade for a second.'

She took the crook of his arm and they walked back to the shadow under the scarecrow. There was a breeze, and Ed felt a little more steady.

'It's hot, isn't it?' she said, and shot an amused glance up at the scarecrow. Dry straw poked out of its pink floral nether regions. The girl cocked her head against the sunlight, eyes scanning the pumpkin impaled on its broom pole frame.

Ed flapped his shirt. 'What'd you say your name was?'

'I didn't say,' the girl murmured. 'It's Danielle.' She was looking at the scarecrow's neck. Yellowish-white, the triangle point of a vertebrae flashed under the pumpkin.

'Wrong—that's wrong.' Ed stuck the barrel of his gun between her shoulder blades, over her heart. 'You're Jenny now.'

No birds scattered. Danielle fell on her face, but it didn't matter. Ed rummaged roughly in her back pockets for the keys to her van, and went to move it off the road.

That was a long night, but Ed enjoyed the work. The next morning he got up with the sun, did the farm jobs as fast as he was able, and stopped to make his sandwich at a quarter past eleven. At noon, he walked out into the field.

'Anyone yet, Jenny?' He grabbed the rainbow deckchair from under her faded, torn pink skirt. He'd cut up those whoreish shorts for oil rags: those were no good. The rest of her was fine. Fly-bait, and fine. He'd gotten the pole right in the sweet spot, pinning her bottom jaw to her palate and keeping her lovely eyes unspoilt for the maggots to nest. Now it'd keep until pumpkin season.

The A4

'And Claire. Give her our love.'

'I will. I will, Uncle Charles.' (Not Charlie... never Charlie. Once, to a "friend" in a bar one night, whose mention, when they thought I was out of earshot, brought a sour, old look onto Aunt Mary's face. Never Charlie... not to anyone else.) His face was round and lined as bread dough, gently sinking under the weight of his own kindness.

I pulled my hand away, and it was immediately sucked into Jill's iron grip. 'Safe journey.'

I'd started saying goodbye about an hour ago. My grin was now rictus: I couldn't help draw morbid parallels. Only two reasons ever made our family gather in my grandmother's musty chintz-stuffed house: christenings, and funerals.

'Thanks. I will.' Jesus, that sounded rude. 'Barring any more accidents on the A4...' I stammered through a rehearsed script: the weather, the traffic, that one good service station with... yes, those pies! *So* good. I'd picked up a fresh one on the way, in a warm plastic packet speckled with condensation. It sat in the car, waiting. God, I'm starving. Home soon.

All the while my eyes scanned the room for hope. God, did somebody light a cigarette in here? Or could I just not remember that room without a thin veil of nicotine clinging like Spanish moss on the curtains?

My cousin Lina's eyes locked on. A small, sad smile played on my rescuer's lips as she hoiked her stodgy toddler higher on her black polyester hips and came over. 'You leaving, Stu?'

I did that closed-mouth, arched-eyebrows smile that screamed *help me*.

'It was good to see you. Maybe—'

'—Better circumstances, next time,' Uncle Charles half-rejoined.

Jill hmm'd in agreement as the vague, crow-like form of Aunt Mary loomed behind Charles. He felt it, and flinched.

'Best be off,' someone mumbled, perhaps him. I didn't hear. I was lost, searching for Mary's face, under a… veil? I couldn't quite see, I felt myself rising on tiptoes. The face of the short, stern lady was always below his shoulder.

'Yes, we best be off as well.' Lina's voice cut through the thick air. Her perfume lingered. 'Drive safe.'

Jill moved closer to me and I felt her hand brush against mine. 'You'll let us know when you get there?'

'Sorry, I…' My head felt light and heavy, all at once. I was drawn into a one-armed embrace from Lina. Her toddler's warm, sweet breath oozed beneath my collar.

'Drive safe.'

'I… I will,' I squeeze her back, not nearly as hard as I want to. 'Are you okay?'

She pulls away from me, warm and sticky, moist. The smell of bread dough and stale smoke fills my nostrils, mingled with her perfume. I feel sick.

There is silence. For a minute, two hours. I don't know how long.

'Best be going.' That was Uncle Charles—I think? His voice

breaks like he's been at the gin. 'I told Mary I'd call when I left.'

'How's she feeling?' asked Jill. 'Shame she couldn't make it.'

'Stu—when you get there—please give all our best to the lovely Claire.' that was Lina, maybe Jill.

I can't see them now. My relatives blur into smoke... rushing beneath me, filling my head, the grey nothingness of the A4. I loll forward into it. My skull is trying slip out from under my skin and the white lines blip, blip like a life support machine. I take a huge gulp of air like a swimmer and surface.

'Look, I really better be off...' I swallow, hard. 'I don't feel great.' Those last four words fade to nothing.

A hand slips around my waist once again. 'Best be off, Stu.'

It's Claire. Her voice melts into a screech of brakes, and a scream. I smell hot meat, in a smear across the windshield. Condensation speckles inside the glass.

'...Wish it could have been better circumstances.'

I hug all of my relatives goodbye. It feels like I've been here for hours, but in reality it's only minutes. Years will pass before I'm here again, and the realisation of how long that time will feel stretches out in front of me like a road with no end. They all smell of the curtains in my grandmother's house, but it's fading now. Their faces are fading.

All of a sudden, I know that smell of smoke is wrong—burning plastic, not my grandmother's nicotine. The smell of meat is not lamb, it's something else.

'Safe journey.'

I open my eyes before I realise they had been clamped shut, and swimmingly make out the mass of what's left of Claire in the passenger seat, gently smouldering. Pain rushes my body as blue and red lights flash in front of me—she stayed. But I made it home.

New Patio

'Mummy? Mummy... It's Joan.'

Gripping the receiver in a flour-dusted hand, Miranda's heart stopped.

'I'm cold. Where's Daddy?'

'Darling—' Her husband, Paul, came in from the kitchen drying his hands.

'I've got the right number, haven't I?'

Miranda's eyes locked on him, signalling for help like a stranded goldfish, soundlessly mouthing. Paul whipped the tea towel over his shoulder and snatched the phone out of her hand.

'Who is this?'

Their daughter had been missing for a week. The lilting, strong voice on the phone was hers—the call neighbours, friends, relatives had been praying for since last Sunday. In the brief silence, Miranda went towards the fireplace. On the mantle sat a pink teddy, notes pinned to plastic flowers and a Guides badge propped against a tealight holder in the shape of an angel.

'J-Joanybean?' The colour drained from Paul's face. 'It can't be you.' He'd used the same voice to explain why rain meant they couldn't go to the park.

'Can I come home? It's dark here.'

Miranda's hands tumbled over each other, rubbing the goose fat and the flour from her knuckles, scraping it from under her fingernails. It was Sunday, and it it had been Sunday one week ago on the 20th, when they had their last family roast. Joan was allowed a second helping—one last treat—before she was told to go outside and help her father take out the old tree stump.

'Sorry, love, what was that?' Paul walked to the French doors. His voice was sturdier, sceptical. He fingered open the vertical blinds and looked out over the new patio. 'I didn't do anything to you, sweetheart. What a horrid thing to say...'

Miranda clapped a hand to her mouth. Paul shot her a look, and motioned violently for her to check the back door.

The kitchen was warm, and smelled of pork. Miranda stumbled through it into the garden. Outside, the new concrete patio oozed within the confines of its ad-hoc plywood mould. The patio they'd poured over cold, lifeless Joan.

Looking up, she saw Paul at the French doors with the phone. His eyes small and dark, he jabbed a finger at the concrete outside, mouthing something. Miranda neared the spot where the stump used to be, fell to her knees and thrust her outstretched hands into the cloying substance.

Paul scrutinised her progress as she crawled through the wet concrete, searching, groping. Finding nothing.

On her signal, Paul's voice reverberated the double glazing. 'I don't know who you are, you bastard, but this is not funny.' He hung up and threw the receiver behind him, onto the sofa.

Miranda heaved an intake of breath she'd been saving and stood up, soaked to the waist in new patio. She and Paul exchanged a look, and behind the double glazing she saw him lace his fingers on top of his head. On her skin, the concrete on her was rapidly hardening. She started to wade out.

The back door slammed shut. Miranda baulked at the noise, and let out a scream at the sight of wet concrete footprints headed inside.

The River Killer

The Ritual of a Thousand Suns hit my desk with a thump. I lowered my cold coffee, and thumbed the stack of pages. 'What's this?'

Price was pacing. 'Accessed one hour ago from public library servers, computer 34. It's his motive.'

I rose to stand in that airless room, our conversation witnessed by the eyes of twenty-three dead women and two men, their photographs pinned to the wall alongside case notes and interview transcripts. Hurriedly, I scanned the printed pages for any mention of a stone relic. 'No, no—we're tracking his home computer, his phone—his shift ends at 9...'

'Swapped last minute,' said Price. 'Only flagged because he used his sixth victim's library card. Charlie...' He placed two open palms on my desk. 'Computer 34 sits by the window overlooking Arlington Heights.'

Price and I ran out of the station into the night.

The media had struggled to name this one, settling most recently on the River Killer. A bogeyman, terrorising the city for months, he'd broken into homes and left messy scenes, seemingly at random. We narrowed in on some suspects, but let them all go. After another batch of killings we found new suspects and revisited old ones... but with little evidence, interviews were ham-fisted. He'd gone quiet. We were praying for a break—at worse, one more corpse.

Last week, we got one.

He botched it, and she fought. A smear of his blood on a broken window matched a recurring suspect.

And that's when things started to fit. This guy knew every single one of his victims—but at first, not so well. Connections were tenuous. But every batch of killings brought him closer. Like concentric rings, the killer was circling acquaintances, then friends, then his loved ones, picking them off one by one. The last had been his sister. Six months ago, his ex-wife had moved to Arlington Heights.

It seemed ridiculous, but we were running out of other motives. Price didn't like it, and neither did I, but the killings were ritualistic. He was appeasing something... some god, or force, we couldn't identify.

As the patrol car sped towards a situation where we didn't yet know the outcome, I couldn't help lock my eyes on the night sky between the tall buildings and wonder what the hell kind of god was worth killing everyone you loved.

A few minutes later, Price held up two fingers and nodded at the team with the battering ram. He glanced at me and I braced, the hardened shell of armour pinching my side as I held up my gun.

'Police! On the ground!'

The cheap door exploded inward, splintering across the hallway of the flat. We entered with deliberate loudness, but we were too late. The ex-wife was bloodied and lifeless at the bottom of the stairs, our prime suspect standing over her.

'It didn't work... it didn't work!' Babbling, a thread of drool fell onto the bug-eyed bastard's shirt. 'Why doesn't it stop?'

Price screamed for him to drop on his knees. Pathetic, he complied, dropping what he had in his hands: a knife, and a stone.

'No one left...' he moaned. My shaking hands kept a gun trained on him as Price put his surrendered hands in cuffs and the other guys swept the flat. 'All gone... didn't work, I failed... I don't love *myself*, how could I...? Why couldn't I do it?' His voice rose to a shriek, tugging at Price.

'Call it self-preservation, you shit,' Price muttered, and hauled him to his feet. I didn't notice. My eyes were fixed on the stone. It was glowing, quietly pulsing.

'You...' The pathetic specimen the newspapers called the River Killer saw me. 'You can help! Listen to me: the only way to destroy it is to sacrifice everything you love! Everyone! Don't touch it—I swear, I loved them! Write it down! I swear!'

'Hey!' Price was wrestling with him now. I snapped my attention back into the room, and reflexed my gun, stepping out of his path.

'Do it!' The River Killer screamed. 'Kill me! Kill... *it!*'

He wrenched himself from Price's grasp, and before anyone could stop him, he was nearly on me. I shot.

The bastard fell on top of me, on the carpet, five feet from his ex-wife. He didn't move. Groaning, I pushed him off, and Price helped me to my feet.

'That's that,' he muttered, over the gently babbling radios. 'Killed twelve people over a fucking shiny pebble. They just get crazier.'

'All loved ones?'

'From the till girl he fancied to his favourite bus driver,' Price said, shaking his head. 'Including his sister and ex-wife. Guess the ritual's complete.'

He clapped my shoulder and headed off to talk with another officer. Massaging my undoubtedly sprained wrist, I looked at the stone on the floor. It was shaking, vibrating, and then it was quiet and cold. Just a stone.

I stooped to pick it up. In my hand, it began glowing. I felt how powerful, how monstrous it was, the things it had seen. I knew I had to get rid of it.

Quietly, it told me how.

Undone

Government officials took notice when reports flooded in of cars failing to start. Then, they started all at once. Birds dropped dead out of the sky. We all had ringing in our ears.

Climate crisis, pandemic, fuel emergency, terrorist attack—all these phrases sound so laughably normal now, antiques in the media cycle. Cause and effect. Relics of a time (a few weeks ago, or was it... no. Sorry. Time is the one thing I struggle letting go of) when any emergency had a response.

It—this, our situation—fragmented off normality. As a scientist, that is so important. I write it everywhere. It began, once. It's easy to forget. It was not always, but it is no longer new. It began with failing to start cars, and birds. Later, altered photographs we could not explain. Bees—oh Christ, millions of bees, and a new species of insect no one could identify. It began with multiples, or variables, on the theme of life.

Then, reality began to splinter.

Arguments began to start about if these new animals were in fact new, or some awful manifestation of the Mandala Effect where we as a collective race simply forgot their existence. All at once, the western world remembered a type of grey speckled rock that was everywhere in their childhoods, but could no longer be found on earth. Online communities compared notes on what was real and what was not.

It happened in real life. Once our memories were infiltrated, it began to use our present reality as a weapon. A boy in Central Park got stuck in one violent millisecond halfway inside a tree: it had grown around his innards, at least sixty rings. His screams were heard for miles. His mother ran to help, and fell up to her waist in sidewalk.

Out of everything, we thought we had science. Facts were failing: on the internet, a subculture hungrily watching for "glitches in the matrix" were overwhelmed with occurrences, spilling out into "this is what's happening". Tables became liquid. Abraham Lincoln was fact, then fiction. Blood ran green, then blue, then according to time of birth, finally invisible and, for some unlucky individuals chosen according to criteria we never identified, became a powder.

Mass panic in the streets. No one knew what was happening, how to predict it, who was responsible or how to get it to stop. All we knew is that we were at the mercy of a world where sixty thousand people could hallucinate a re-enactment of World War II in the space of three minutes, killing millions.

I was given a mission, once I regained my sense of sight which disappeared one Tuesday. Our research was mapped as best we could, but sometimes our memories, our bodies, our environment failed us. Stacks of information would go missing. One woman woke up knowing the cure to cancer, forgot it, and went mad. Ghosts stalked the cafeteria and occasionally melted into brown pools.

As of this moment, there's a quote tattooed on my arm: *"Reality is merely an illusion, albeit a very persistent one."* Einstein. I must have once thought it important.

Anyway. Now, it's obsolete. Any attempt to quantify this, to work out what's going on, is futile. I'm not sure my colleagues ever existed. I'm not sure "exist" is still the benchmark to use.

It fragmented off normality. First, the multiples and the variables, changing colours and quantities and spatial locations. A container ship, forty feet above the waves, blue wasps. Then, it spiralled outwards like a fractal snowflake, deeper iterations of nonsense, affecting time, memory, gravity... physics.

One day, we've figured it out. The next, billions of us are gone, by happenstance or their own hand. Sometimes, they come back. Increasingly not.

This is how it ends. Not with climate change, but our natural laws collapsing in on each other. But if this is a natural part of the death of the universe, an attack by some unseen force or some unholy bad luck, we have no idea. Either way, human race will soon be blasted from existence by a slip of a cosmic finger.

I'm in Central Park. I lower my notebook and watch the trees racing above me, faster and faster. I sit on nothing. I briefly am a child, a metaphor, then a jaguar, and finally myself, though it's getting more fleeting. I am sure we will figure it out—we have to, but we will never get to figure it out.

I don't think we ever even mattered.

In the Streetlight

It was October and the days were short. The sky was already dark at 6pm and the streetlights had come on while I walked home. The route took me across a small dog park: a square of grass in the middle of houses criss-crossed with paths.

It was fine, until I saw him.

While I planned what to eat for dinner, I'd clocked the black silhouette of a man standing still out of the side of one eye. I thought his dog must have run off. I waited to hear him call its name, but it never came. I kept walking, and got to the path at right angles to his.

The streetlights went off.

I stopped, blinded by the darkness. It wasn't two seconds later they flickered back on.

My senses were at full alert: I could taste metallic fear cutting through the chocolate bar fuzz on my tongue, my heartbeat was rapid and my eyes hurt as they raced to scan my surroundings to check if everything was the same.

Only the black silhouette of the man had advanced twenty feet closer to me on the path.

I fixed him with a stare, too afraid to move. 'Hello?' I called. No answer.

IN THE STREETLIGHT

The streetlights went out, once more. I flinched as the night rushed in around me, and clutched my bag. I didn't know how he was doing it—if he was doing it? What was happening?

Flickering back on, the lights illuminated the man, now visible in a pool of orange light. Unkempt. Wild-eyed. In an old, filthy coat, yellow beard and military boots. Fixing his arms out from his body, breathing heavily, like a stick-man in a game. I heard a fluttering rumble, as if a moth was stuck in my ear. It got louder.

The lights went out.

I could hear his heavy breathing as he ran towards me. I took off down the path away from him, bag swinging at my side, ready to throw it if he got too close. I heard his heavy boot steps rush up to me and pass, barging into me and carrying on.

'Stop!'

He yelled it just as the streetlights came back on. Against my instinct, I froze. He was a few feet in front of me, caught mid-run, still flexed.

We stood there, still.

'What do you want?' I said.

'It sucks energy from the lights,' he whispered.

The fluttering rumble started again, getting incrementally louder. The man turned his yellowed, wide eyes over his shoulder to look at me.

'It can't move in the dark,' he said. 'Run!'

The streetlights went out.

Corpse #2

The noise of rolling metal fills my ears as my drawer is opened and I am pulled out into the light. A milky fluorescent glow burns through my closed eyelids. I am lying on my back, rigid and still.

'How did he die?' said a deep, male voice.

'Multiple laceration wounds, subject bled out,' said a female voice. Warm, plastic fingers slide under my arm and lift it. 'Check out the wrists. Cut to ribbons.'

'Guess he couldn't take the fact he shot his wife in the head last week and buried her in the woods.'

'That's the thing: I don't think it was self-inflicted.'

'What makes you say that?'

'The razor blade found near the body doesn't fit the injury. This incision is jagged, imprecise.' She gently lays down my arm. 'Were there any knives in the house?'

'Only a set of cheap kitchen knives.'

'Any of them missing?'

'One.'

'We need to check the kitchen for prints,' she said, inching open my eye and shining a torchlight straight into it. 'If the killer was in the...' The words died in her throat. 'Knife block. Shit.'

'Cut!' yells a tinny voice from the other end of the studio. '"We need to check the *knife block* for prints, if the killer was in the *kitchen...*"'

'Got it,' she said irritably, and I heard the sound of snapping plastic. 'Can I get a coffee? Is that lunch?'

'That's lunch.'

I screwed my eyes shut, rubbing out the fluorescent glow with a constellation of sparkling lights, and sat up on the gurney. The sheet pooled around the waistband of my flesh-coloured Lycra shorts, which were seamless and wouldn't be visible under the white mortuary sheet.

'Great job, Kathy—' I began to say, but she was already walking off. I didn't think a real pathologist wore heels in the office, and they'd certainly tie up their bouncy waves of hair, but hell—I wasn't wardrobe, I was just an extra. Corpse #2.

I swung my legs over the side of the gurney and wiggled my toes, feeling rushing back into the piggies. It had been a long day. Felt like we'd filmed this scene a hundred times.

I got a styrofoam cup of coffee from the machine—lattes were reserved for talent— and wandered around, doing that closed-mouth arched-eyebrows smile at people who accidentally made eye contact. I guess the hollow-eyed, yellow-skinned corpse makeup was a bit unnerving. I rubbed my cheek, and looked at my fingers. No smear came off. Jesus, had it sunk in? Was I gonna get lead poisoning? I flexed my jaw to get feeling back in it. Laying still for hours at a time was hard work.

No, this wasn't the Hollywood career of my glittering teenage dreams, but it paid the bills and was better than wasting my life in an office. I'd started out in background work, out-of-focus, every so often managing to jostle into frame over the main actor's shoulder. At least now I was on screen for more than half a second, even if the main requirement was to hold my breath. Yoga helped. I was slightly embarrassed to admit it, but I often talked people's ears off about how to play a convincing corpse. It wasn't just a case of lying there and keeping your mouth shut, it's actually pretty interesting: you have to slow your breathing which involves mindfulness and regular meditation, as well as learning how to suppress reflexes. Lately, I'd been practising controlling my eye muscles, which would allow for close-ups that wouldn't need to be fixed in post. Corpse-craft is a demanding mistress. Everyone's gotta have a hobby.

'Hey, when do you think we'll wrap today?' I asked the girl at the monitor, whose headphones rested at her neck. She didn't acknowledge me. Even for Hollywood, that was rude. I walked off.

My last job was better than this, working with Saul Poloski on the set of a thriller about a deadly gas on a train. Although, rigid on a cold chrome gurney was better than slumped awkwardly over a train seat for hours… Jesus, when was that? Six months ago? A year? Time flies.

I stood in the middle of the studio as others milled around me, talking about framing shots, muttering about the industry and touching up powder. I took a sip of coffee. It tasted of absolutely nothing.

'Great day, gang,' I said, loudly. 'I really think we're doing good work here.'

No one noticed me. I'd lifted my wrist halfway to my face before I realised I'd left my wristwatch in the locker. A chemical-smelling crimson gash adorned my wrist like a bracelet, leaving a greasy smear on the styrofoam cup. I swore, and looked around for a makeup who was free.

'Can anybody…? I think I need a touch up,' I called. No

one—not Kathy, not Tom, the lead, or the director, no one—took any notice. I was frustrated. 'Hello?' I called. 'Can I get makeup here? My gash is leaking.'

'Where do you think you are?' It was the headphones girl, by the monitor. She hadn't gotten to her feet, just twisted around to face me.

I looked at her, confused. 'Sorry?' There was a pause. 'I'm... my name is, uh...' What the fuck. Why couldn't I remember? I blurted out, 'Corpse #2.'

'Yeah. I know,' she said.

At that moment I realised that everyone—the actors, makeup, wardrobe and all peripheral technicians working on the show—had stopped, and their eyes were fixed on me. Silent. I whipped my head around, feeling crazy. What the fuck was wrong with everyone?

'All right people, back on set,' said a disembodied, tinny voice. Everyone jerked into motion, as if someone had pressed Play.

'What's... seriously, what's going on?' I felt a rising sense of panic. Coldness settled in the pit of my stomach. 'No. Oh God... how long have I been here?'

As they all got into their positions, the girl heaved a sigh and unwrapped the headphones from her neck. 'You're needed on set. We need another take.'

'No,' I whispered. My arm fell by my side, spilling bad coffee all over the floor. A runner was immediately on it with a rag. 'No. I won't.'

'Please, sir. Get onto the gurney, and someone will close the drawer.'

'I c-can't,' I said, backing away. 'Don't make me. Please.'

But I backed too far, and went over the tape onto the vinyl flooring into the brightly-lit morgue set. Two runners grabbed my arms with crimson smears. 'Get off me!' I screamed, wriggling out of their grasp. 'Can we just stop for a minute—I need some air, I want to go home!'

'Then you shouldn't have killed your wife,' said the girl with a shrug, pulling her headphones back on and turning back to the monitor.

The runners were too strong. They wrestled me onto the gurney, yanked my legs straight, and I couldn't sit up as they pushed me halfway inside.

'How many takes do you need?' I choked, as my vision was reduced to a small, white square containing the makeup-plastered faces of the two actors. They said nothing as the drawer was slammed closed with a metallic clang.

Again, and for the upteenth time for all eternity, we restarted the scene.

The Red Man

I'm 28, they tell me —and they love to repeat it. What am I doing wasting away in an office, Karen crows? Should be out partying, Linda says, touching a limp hand on my shoulder with what she hopes is a vivacious smile. It's smeared with too much lipstick. They're in their fifties and they have more of a life than me.

After about six hours, the spreadsheets make my eyes cross. I'm trying to get to seven. I got this job, and I won't let it go. I need a promotion. I don't need to party.

I tried to explain to Mum why I wasn't spending as much time with her, how I just didn't "have evenings" like her friends' sons who still lived at home, and why it was so important I "chose" the office. But her lips made a taut, straight line and she looked like she was going to cry. I never chose the office over her. No, she was first. I was putting her above all else. I had to, because the nightmare looming on the horizon had chosen *me*.

I'm the one who gets the dishwasher fixed. I'm the one who replaces the milk. Mum says, 'Oh, I've got change, I'll get it when I'm next at the shops,' but she's lying about having the money. I make sure I get to it first, and I don't say a word. But when my eyes start to swim at the office at 7.30pm when I attempt a double shift, I see our chipped, yellowed Formica countertops and rusted hob, I see our threadbare carpet and the cardboard over the bathroom vent. I see the state my father left us in... and I'm angry, but not at him.

I was six years old. He was 31. And he lasted all of six months of it, before he tore the cheek off his face and ran screaming onto the M8.

'I am so sorry,' Karen cooed, when I told her—in an edited version—why I wasn't doing anything special with my parents for my birthday. 'Well don't you worry. It's tradition to do birthdays here!'

I didn't have the heart to say no.

After it happened, we struggled. I to make sense of it, Mum to make ends meet. She'd never said a word of what he saw at the end: my aunt had to explain it to me. How horrific it was when her father, my grandfather, died at 31.

How it took them two days to locate all the parts.

The bruises still on his knuckles from the homemade bars on the windows.

Ten months of screaming.

How he'd always wanted an open casket, and how that was impossible.

In a shaking voice, I asked her what was wrong with his face? She said no, she didn't mean that: they couldn't find *enough* of him for a casket. They buried him in a wet shoebox.

The Red Man had come for him, as he does to all the oldest boys when they turn 31.

It sounds like a random number, but then I learned a few generations before me had pieced it together, traced it in libraries and through case numbers, and they think it goes back to my great-great-grandfather who spent four years in jail at age 31 for the murder of a railroad worker over gambling debts (he'd been sentenced to nine). Soon after he was locked in his cell, he began complaining of seeing a man, red from head to toe, as if he was on fire. The guards didn't believe him, and my great-great-grandfather got irate, then maddened, and then he turned violent. Screamed that the Red Man was burning his skin and stealing his mind.

The guards and other inmates endured four years of his ranting and screaming, until they found him hanging.

I think of this and smile blandly whenever Linda shows me pictures of her grandchildren. I'm already 28, I won't ever see any of mine. Neither did the railroad worker: his burnt corpse was discovered on the tracks, drenched in gasoline fumes.

I'm the oldest, an only child. My father cried when he found out I was a boy, because he'd already been seeing the man in fleeting glimpses, and for the six months he was alive after age 31 I witnessed the Red Man taking over and my father slowly go mad. Two mornings before he killed himself I saw him cut himself while shaving, and his eyes went as big as dinner plates when he saw the blood. He started smearing it over his face, until he was all red. Then he fixed his gaze on something he saw over his shoulder in the mirror, but it wasn't me.

I work in this office for ten hours a day, sometimes twelve. I will be promoted in three months, and that will mean I earn £4,000 a year extra. Enough to get new carpets. I've been saving forty percent of my income since my first job delivering leaflets at age eleven. I've been working since, every minute possible.

Dad left her with nothing: I won't. Mum won't ever have grandchildren: my workload has seen to that, not that I've ever dared to even consider it. The Red Man will come for me, but she'll have enough to live on when the inevitable happens, and there won't be anyone after me.

I sit at my keyboard, my hands resting in my lap. It's nearly five, my eyes are swimming, and the formulas on screen have melted. This is how I sleep, and I dream of a song... it gets closer, and in the screen's reflection I see Karen and Linda, either side of me with others singing Happy Birthday.

I get up, and smile. I blow out my candles, and say thank you. They do frowny smiles when I confirm that yes, I'm staying, and no, I haven't any plans. Over their shoulders, I spot the outline of a blood-hued man on the edge of reality. Vague platitudes come forth, and a few minutes later they've left the office to go home for the evening and I sit in front of my computer with a slice of red velvet cake.

I am 29. I don't have long left.

The Flogsta Scream

In Flogsta, the echoes of overworked students' howls echo in the city's cold and starry night.

The first time I heard it, I was beside myself. No one had told me. I only saw Anna's beautiful face crease up, a theatre mask of comedy above her mug of cocoa, at odds with the horrifying noise that floated through the sash window we'd lifted, at her flatmates' insistence.

I was just a freshman. If Anna's hot hand hadn't squeezed my wrist, I would have run for my coat.

From then on, our twice-weekly intensive night-time study sessions were split in half by the scream. At approximately ten in the evening, every night, the traditional Flogsta echo galvanises the black and fluorescent orange snowy streets as students let out their frustrations from windows, balconies and rooftops.

Anna and I took a walk one night, before exams, to hear it properly and scream ourselves. I'd read an official statement by Uppsala University that explained the act as "a much-needed safety valve" that prevented the earnest future academics of Sweden from blowing their brains out. A good old scream helps the soul, Anna told me.

It's a mass hysteria that has spread to Lund, Linköping and the

Lappkärrsberget. It wasn't long before I was a regular screamer, as our final year drew near. Cardiology is not a forgiving subject. Lectures were a slog, and the coursework relentless. It wasn't long before a nightly scream no longer helped.

I had to find something else.

'You need more practical experience,' my lecturer said. 'Theoretical discourse can only take you so far, and you're past that point.'

'How do I get more practical experience?' I cried, exasperated. I had not been accepted into any hospitals. Unpaid work was thin on the ground, fought over by students like starving wolves. My lecturer shrugged.

It was Anna who gave me the solution. Dear, sweet Anna.

The first time I did it, her hands were so warm. They gripped my wrists. I saw Anna's heavenly face crease into a mask of horror as I plunged the fish knife into her chest, her choked wails muffled by the howls from the chilling screams that poured from the balconies, roof-tops and open windows of Flogsta student flats.

I keep the window open as I dissect her heart and sip my cocoa, greasy and shimmering in the reflection of the night-time lights. I pull apart the veins and aorta, marvelling at the loveliness of her internal workings. I know soft tissue won't last long, even in the fridge.

But hey, the Flogsta scream happens every night. I can hunt whenever I want.

About the Author

Beth Scott is a copywriter and horror enthusiast whose hobbies include knitting, true crime, historical landscapes and the unexplained. She lives in the West of Scotland with her husband and beloved wool stash.

You can connect with me on:
- http://www.brscottauthor.com

Printed in Great Britain
by Amazon